NORMAN BRIDWELL

Clifford's®
HAPPY MOTHER'S DAY

SCHOLASTIC INC

New York   Toronto   London   Auckland   Sydney

Mexico City   New Delhi   Hong Kong

To Tatsuo Parker Bridwell

The author thanks Manny Campana
for his contribution to this book.

ISBN: 0-439-22229-X
Copyright © 2001 by Norman Bridwell.
All rights reserved. Published by Scholastic Inc.
SCHOLASTIC, CARTWHEEL BOOKS and associated logos are trademarks and/or registered trademarks of Scholastic Inc.
CLIFFORD, CLIFFORD THE SMALL RED PUPPY, CLIFFORD THE BIG RED DOG, and associated logos are trademarks
and/or registered trademarks of Norman Bridwell.

Library of Congress Cataloging-in-Publication Data available

10 9 8 7 6 5 4 3 2 1   01 02 03 04 05

Printed in the U.S.A.
First printing, April 2001

When I was little, my family lived in the city.

My dog, Clifford, was born in the apartment next door.

He was the smallest puppy in the litter.

Because he was so small, his mother took special care of him.

That's me, Emily Elizabeth.

One day our neighbor called us. He wanted to give me a puppy.

He told me to choose one.

You know which one I took.

When Mother's Day came, Clifford and I wanted
to get something special for my mom.

Daddy took us to the candy store to get her some chocolates.

While I was choosing chocolates, Clifford saw a ribbon on a box of candy.

Clifford loves to play with ribbons.

Oh dear! We decided to buy the candy Clifford chose.

Daddy paid the candy store owner and we went
on to the flower shop.

I picked out a nice bunch of flowers for my mom.

Flowers make Clifford sneeze.

He had a big sneeze for such a tiny dog. We decided to buy the flowers he had sneezed on.

Now we had enough presents.
But I still needed a card.

Daddy said I should make the card myself.

We could buy paper and decorations in the store.

I picked out some paper.

Clifford chose the decorations.

I went to work as soon as we got home.

Clifford watched me closely.

He came a little *too* close.

He couldn't see where he was going.
What a mess!

I unglued Clifford, but my card was ruined.
Now I had to start over again.

I got another idea.

STAMP PAD

I signed the card
with my handprint.

I forgot to close the top
of the stamp pad.

That was a mistake.

What would Mommy say when she saw
Clifford's paw prints all over my sweater?

The next day we gave Mom her presents.

She loved them all.

She told me not to worry about the sweater.

She knew just what to do.

We took it next door to Clifford's mother.

My sweater fit inside her basket.

Now she had a Mother's Day gift, too.

Even though Clifford is all grown up,
he's still his mother's little puppy.